# Little Seahorse
## and the
# Big Storm

**by Anne Giulieri**
illustrated by Omar Aranda

A big storm made the waves
go up and down.
"Oh, no!" cried Little Sea Horse.
And the big waves
took her away from home.

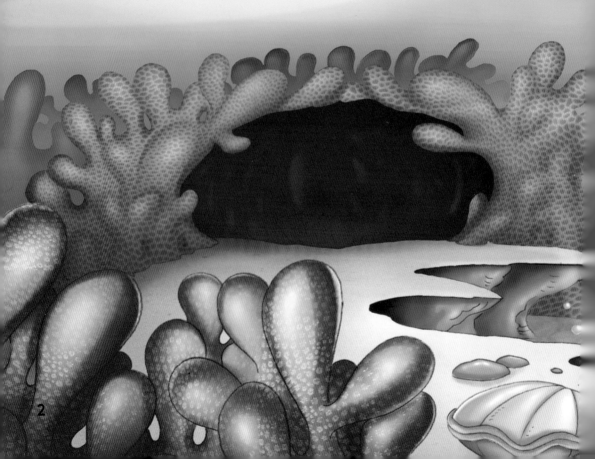

The big waves
went up and down.
Little Sea Horse
went over and under.
She was scared.

"Oh, dear!" cried Little Sea Horse.
"I want to go home."

"Hello, Little Sea Horse,"
said Dolphin.
"I'm a long way from home, too."

The big waves
went up and down.
Little Sea Horse and
Dolphin went over
and under.

"I'm scared,"
cried Little Sea Horse.

"I'm scared, too," said Dolphin.
"Come and swim next to me.
We can swim into the cave."

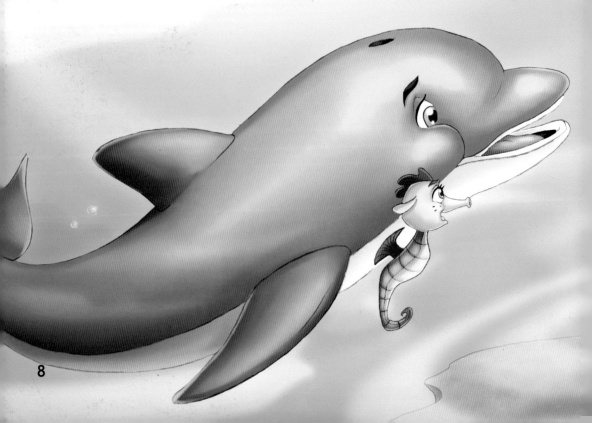

It was safe inside the cave.
"I'm happy you are with me,"
said Little Sea Horse.

"I'm happy you are
with me, too," said Dolphin.

Little Sea Horse looked out.
"Can we go home?"
asked Little Sea Horse.
"The waves are not big.
The storm is over."

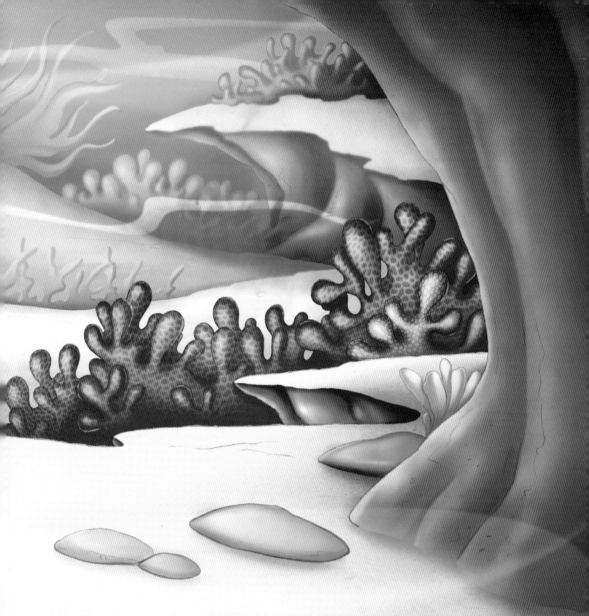

"Yes," said Dolphin.

"You can swim next to me."

Little Sea Horse
saw Father Sea Horse.
"I was lost in the storm,"
she said.
"Dolphin helped me
to swim home."

"I'm so happy to see you,"
said Father Sea Horse.
"And I'm happy
to see you too, Dolphin."